The Smallest Gift of CHRISTMAS

PETER H. REYNOLDS

CANDLEWICK PRESS

Roland was eager for Christmas Day.

He raced downstairs to see what
was waiting for him.

But when he saw his present,
he was not impressed.
It was the smallest gift
he had <u>ever</u> seen.
Had he waited the whole year
for this tiny gift?

Roland closed his eyes and hoped
and wished as hard as he could
for a BIGGER gift.

And when he opened his eyes,
there WAS a bigger gift!

"You call THAT big?" Roland asked. He had been wishing for something MUCH bigger. He closed his eyes and wished a little harder.

"Ha! That one isn't much bigger than me," Roland said. "And <u>I'm</u> not very big!"

A BIGGER GIFT!"

"BIG? That's not even as big as my house! When I say big, I mean BIG!" he yelled.

Roland stomped off, sure there was
a bigger gift for him—<u>somewhere</u>.

In the distance, he saw a present wedged between two buildings.

Now THAT, Roland thought, that is pretty big. But still not big enough!

Roland was determined.

So he set off to search the universe.

He searched and searched, but all he could see were billions of stars.

Roland peered into his telescope.

He could just make out a
tiny dot in the distance.

Earth! His home, his family . . .
now just a speck, growing
smaller and smaller.

Roland realized that he was very,
VERY far from home and that
if he waited a heartbeat longer,
that little dot would disappear.

Roland never thought he'd want
something so small so badly.

He closed his eyes and hoped and wished with all his might for that tiny speck — the smallest gift.

As the rocket headed toward it,
the dot grew bigger and bigger.

1

As Roland's rocket landed gently,

he realized that the smallest speck
<u>was</u> his biggest gift.

Roland was home.

Merry Christmas!

To Henry Rocket Reynolds

First edition in this format 2015

Library of Congress Catalog Card Number 2012947753
ISBN 978-0-7636-6103-8 (original hardcover)
ISBN 978-0-7636-7981-1 (midi hardcover)

15 16 17 18 19 20 APS 10 9 8 7 6 5 4 3 2 1

Printed in Humen, Dongguan, China

This book was hand-lettered by Peter H. Reynolds.
The illustrations were created digitally.

Candlewick Press
99 Dover Street
Somerville, Massachusetts 02144

visit us at www.candlewick.com